The Cottage That

Stood Alone

By

Annie Hughes

Chapter 1

Run.

The word bellowed in my head, reaching a louder and louder echo. I could hear the word so vividly that images sprung to my congested mind-distorted images of me running- running through the woods of trees upon trees. The enormous land was pulled together by leaves that as I ran along, floated in the air. My breath began to quicken along with my heart which was beating immensely fast. The stump which lay upon the ground was hidden in the darkness, my feet toppled on top of one another leaving my body pounding to the floor.

I couldn't move, nor could I speak, the only movement was the gasps from my troubled breath rebounding through the woods, as I lay with my head facing towards the floor my breath beginning to slow down and my body temperature coming back to normal, I lifted my shoulders upwards to see a direction for an exit. I couldn't think straight- I couldn't see clearly as blood from my head flowed into my vision of the grove in front.

The silence was staggering. Not even a gust of wind that usually rustled the trees was heard. I used my forearms to bring myself up to a steady height, before I had a chance to look back my legs were pulled from beneath me leaving a scream to eject from my body. The scream awoke me from my images but jerked me awake from the same nightmare that recurred nightly. I sprang to an upright position, my hands still in a tight clenched fist my breath was a repeat of the terror I felt in my mind. The cold sweat from my forehead pierced down my eyes leaving a sting to my vision. "Shit" the word wailed out of my mouth leaving Emmett to awake in shock.

"What? What happened?" his soft hazel eyes looked into mine with pity as though he knew exactly what happened.

"Another nightmare?" His deep husky voice came from his gentle smile.

I couldn't find the words to respond. I just scrunched my hair behind my ears and swiftly nodded my head. He pulled me to his chest whilst wrapping his manly arms around my face stroking the wisps of hair. He knew how to handle situations so much better than me, sometimes I didn't know what was even wrong and yet he just gave me that comforting smile which was his way of saying 'everything will be fine.'

Just as my eyes began to feel heavy Emmett said sternly "Don't forget you have your first counselling session at the medical clinic at ten today."

The whole atmosphere in the room changed as though a cold shiver was sent through my spine...

"Just remember if you need me for these sessions, I will get the time off work."

"No, no I'll be fine I'm just going to get back to sleep" I said with the fakest smile upon my lips.

I rolled over to the other side sliding my jaws side to side as a distraction from the upcoming counselling session. I wasn't the best at talking about my feelings in any kind of way but I knew when the dreaded question would be asked, I'd have to talk about that night.

The next morning was a blur. If I'm honest I was that tired, I don't know how I made it into the building. I made it to the top floor where the numerous rooms were lined in rows. I'd never been to counselling before, I didn't really know what to expect.

The receptionist smiled as I drew closer to the table "Are you here to see Melanie?" Her voice was so soft and elegant as she greeted me.

"Yes", I replied with a slightly reluctant tone.

"What's your name please?" she questioned

"Bethany, Bethany Pryon", the words staggered out of my mouth.

"Okay if you'd like to take a seat in the waiting area and Melanie will be with you shortly" she replied sympathetically.

"Thank you, please can you tell me where the toilets are?" My voice betrayed me as the words came out in a nervous tone.

"Of course, just straight down the hall and to the right" her head faced back to the computer.

"Thankyou".

Walking down the hall my head peering through each slight bend in the wall, the hallway itself was long and felt never-ending. My eyes were drawn to look above to the spotlights which were engraved into the ceiling, the aureate glow had such a demanding manner that it made me realise the hall seemed so abnormal. Not only did the length seem so excessive but it felt too big to fit in such a small place. Finally, from what felt like an eternity the doors for the toilets stood to the right-hand side.

I slowly opened the door to the ladies. I noted ahead of me in front of each sink were tall polished mirrors as I looked in the one directly opposite me where I caught a glimpse of the dark rings under my eyes. I reached for my concealer out of my bag when a sharp light pierced through my eyes forcing me to close them, a vision was racing through my mind almost like a flashback. I reached my hands forward to the sink, scooping up the water and splashing my eyes to be able to regain my sight. I looked back to the mirror, the water gliding down my hands dripping off my fingertips. I couldn't see what the image in my mind was but I knew it was something to fear. I painted the concealer under my eyes, blending it through to my cheeks, covering the rings to match my pale skin colour.

As I made my way back to the hallway, I reached the door of the waiting room but there didn't appear to be anyone else in there. The waiting room was empty and eerily quiet. The wall was painted with a shade of cloud grey with matching furniture of a slightly darker grey, a white coffee table was placed in front with the latest magazines about the social gossip of the world, I could distinctly remember my teenage years of reading through magazines trying to imagine what life's like for the people on the front covers and picturing myself in that situation. When I was younger, I was a bit of an outsider, I didn't have many friends for that type of girly gossip, the only way I could change that was to write fantasy books putting myself as the princess who gets rescued by my knight in shining armour and imagining my future which is yet to come, the ironic think if only my past self could see what an amazing prince I ended up with.

 My silent thoughts were broken from the echoing screech of a door opening, from behind the door came a woman who looked straight upon my direction

"You must be Mrs. Pryon".

Chapter 2

I was sitting in what could only be described as a box room, lifeless in colour, just pure white surrounding walls. The room was plain and bare but very aesthetic in that it was filled with plants on each table and on the desk, exotic paintings which appeared to have stories behind them decorated the bland walls.

Melanie walked and sat at her desk, she had short, brown, neat hair with streaks of golden blonde, her fringe reached all the way down to her eyebrows which lead to the freckles trickling down through her nose to her cheeks. Her red rosy cheeks matched the colour to her lips which were still smiling directly to me. Her outfit was so sophisticated, she wore a white shirt with blue lines paired with a black skirt which sounds formal yet she carried it so well.

"Hello Mrs Pryon my name is Melanie, hopefully I'll be able to help you to deal with any trauma and help relieve your stress levels with the appropriate therapy, but the first thing I'd like to do is ask you what has brought you to therapy? I know you've been referred and I have gone through your doctor's notes but I'd like to ask how you feel about this and where you would like to start?" Melanie spoke with a calm demeanour.

"Bethany is fine, Mrs. Pryon sounds a bit formal" I implied.

Melanie responded with a slight laugh, and nodded in a way that felt like she understood, "okay Bethany."

At that moment I just froze. I wasn't sure where to even start. The only words I could stagger out uncomfortably were the murmurs of the noise…. erm.

Finally, Melanie broke the awkwardness "Let me make this easier, I can see from your past reports from your doctor that a cottage has been mentioned throughout, how about we start from there."

The words after the cottage didn't seem to sink in, I felt my eyes fix on the bit of sunlight which shone through the stained-glass window. My eyes remained completely zoned out but my mouth was overtaken with words that just appeared to roll out.

"I remember the date, to be exact it was the seventeenth of June the day me and my husband bought our first house, we always dreamed of the idea of a cosy quaint place that we could call our own," a small smile emerged from my gaze thinking of the life we had made for ourselves.

"Okay let's start with that point, tell me about the first day you moved to the cottage."

"It was two weeks after our wedding we'd just got back off our honeymoon in Greece, which I thought nothing could compete with , but then knowing we were returning to our own home where life would be just as wonderful for us had such an immense sense of not only

8

achievement that we'd both met our soulmates, but excitement of the unknown, little did I know what the unknown had in store for me."

"Outside the cottage there was a view like no other. My arms laid softly upon the wooden fence, my fingers moving with the wind, my hair wisped along my leather jacket catching upon my fair eyelashes. My eyes gazed upon the shades of blue that illuminated the land beneath me where the sand was pulled to join the sea as the waves folded into the distance. I closed my eyes to fully enjoy the harmonious surroundings and to embrace this warm feeling. In this moment everything felt blissfully comforting in the fact that this would be my life from now on. I looked out to that beautiful crystal sea and imagined the rest of our lives together watching our own children play in the sea for many long blissful hours. I could see as clear as day the picture of Emmitt's face as he strolled over to where I was standing watching over the sea. ' I know that smile , what you thinking about?' Emmett said watching me as I gazed out in the open. 'I'm just taking it all in, such a tranquil, peaceful place like we always dreamed of.' By this point Emmett had his arms wrapped around me , his chin resting on my head as we both looked out to the sea."

"Sounds like everything was perfect," Melanie's smile had turned to pity.

At this point I was suddenly shaken out of my daydream as my eyes regained consciousness from the images in my head back to the room where I was sitting. "That's a really good start Bethany. I can feel the emotion in your words and I can tell by the way you described it all." Melanie sat calmly nodding for me to continue. I paused long and hard trying to find the words to describe the next part of that very day.

As the silence hung in the air Melanie casually dropped her head down and focused on the book where she was writing down my story but probably in her own words. I mean how could she even begin to describe my story with the same amount of emotion I was feeling?

Again it was Melanie who broke the silence.

" I'm really happy with the progress we've made already and I'm really pleased you've had the courage to even come here today" I didn't respond, just nodded my head in agreement slightly feeling like she was just saying that to make me feel better.

" I'd like two sessions a week for now if that's okay with you? Your husband mentioned the recurring nightmares you have when I spoke to him, he said they happen most nights is that right?" She looked questioningly at me as though she was unsure of what my response would be.

" Oh , I didn't know you spoke to my husband," my eyebrows folded into a deep frown.

" Yes, he mentioned that last week you had what he said he believed to be a breakdown, not knowing where you was or who he was so he suggested that you have two sessions a week for now until we can prevent such feelings coming on and how to deal with them, sorry I thought he would have told you" a shocked sound sprang through her voice.

"No I haven't had a chance to properly speak to him yet" My response didn't in any way deflect what I was thinking, it didn't dawn on me he would be discussing my problems with this woman I just assumed he'd rang to make an appointment and would let me tell her what happened in my own way and own time. The rational side of me kicked in and I assumed he didn't discuss it with me because my reaction would have probably been a negative attitude to his suggestion as it just was.

"So our next session will be on Wednesday at noon and if you need me before then here's my card. It has my work number on there so if you ever need to talk just give me a ring" she said, handing me a small pocket-sized card.

" Thank you," I quietly replied.

" Your welcome, I'll see you Wednesday and well done today, these sessions will get easier and we'll take one step at a time together."

I smiled in response as I couldn't find the words to reply and with that, I opened the door from the room back to the hallway.

Stepping from the revolving door, the wind felt like a gale swaying my whole body from side to side, how weird I don't remember the weather being this bad when I went into the building. Turning through to the Highgate the street was buzzing with the hustle and bustle of people going in and out of shops, mind you in this weather I'm surprised people could keep control of the paper bags they gripped onto fiercely.

I merely glanced into each shop peering from one end of the window to another, I didn't feel like shopping today. I was too weary. I didn't feel like my feet could carry me much longer, note to self - heeled boots and no sleep don't really mix. I started my staggered walk home turning through the side street of Highgate.

As I turned the corner I came upon a person who was stood in a forceful position ,his hands clenched straining both his arms, his legs stood apart in line with his hips at a slight bend. He was wearing all black. His jacket smooth textured , the kind of which you could hear each raindrop fall on. His darkly coloured jeans sat just on top of his boots. The boots , the kind of style I fear I recognise. They were worker boots, military style, polished up to scratch. They were so eye-catching due to the owner having at least a shoe size of eleven to twelve.

I didn't let him think I'd acknowledged him and swiftly retraced my steps through the Highgate. I picked up the pace not daring to look back. I couldn't tell if the domineering sounds that seemed to be following me were the sound of footsteps or the sound of my heart thumping through my chest. My quickest reaction was to find the closest coffee shop where there are bound to be people inside. I pounded into the one on the corner slamming the door behind me. The shop froze. Everyone started at me in astonishment as my quivered hands readjusted the hair from within my eyes . My head facing the other way moving as quick as I could to the nearest table. With that the noise suffused through the walls again leaving my breath to blend in with the chatter.

On reflection all I could think about was the boots, I should really be acknowledging the event of what just happened yet all I could think about were the boots, where had I seen them before? Why are they of such importance? No matter how many times I asked the questions I couldn't see the answers but one thing I knew the boots were significant to something or why else would I cling on to such a thought?

I shook my head, my eyes blinking hard. I tried to become cognizant of my surroundings . A couple were sitting next to me , clearly new to their setting. Their excitement and happy smiles reminded me of the first few dates I went on with Emmett and the conversations of what we both wanted out of life, the feeling of shock spread through my body causing a swift jolt. I screwed my eyes to fully comprehend the image that was running through my mind. The boots were as clear as day , in my mind I could see them on the feet of a man . I remember how my body was boiling with anger. I felt as though I was going mad. I was ever so slightly pondering on whether this person was the same man in my kitchen the last night at the cottage. I don't understand, could this be the same man? How on earth did he find me?

Chapter 3

I swear he was there - sinking slowly into the bathtub the water lay motionless under my chin. But the vague sounds of dripping ripples gestured beneath my earlobes.

" I never said he wasn't Bethany I just think that you've been under a lot of stress and I'm worried that you're going to spiral down again" I could hear the frustration coming from Emmett's tone.

"It's not stress, I am more than capable of telling the difference so stop trying to presume what I do and don't know!" I shouted in response.

The echo of my shout lingered from wall to wall of the bathroom which left us both stunned by how loud I could be when I got mad.

"Look, I'm sorry okay, I just never want to see you go through what you did a few weeks ago, I'll never forget the look on your face the day you had the breakdown." Sitting on the edge of the bathtub, he reached for my hand placing his in mine.

" I believe you" he said whilst kissing my head softly. "Are you going to be okay for tomorrow?" My head looked straight at him.

"Tomorrow?" I questioned.

" Chloe's book signing for her new thriller" his eyebrows were raised tightly whilst smiling.

I placed my hand above my head and slid it down to my eyes which were closed.

" I had completely forgotten about that" I bit my teeth into my lip as the anxiety built up in my body.

"We don't have to go ; I'll make up some excuse and we'll have a night in together" Emmett said persuasively.

" I highly doubt your sister would let you get away with not going to the book signing she's been dreaming about ever since she started this book" I smiled at him knowing full well he knew she'd be mortified with him.

" No I'll be fine, anyway it's nice to talk to your sister. She tries to persuade me to start writing and says it's a good way to challenge inner anger," I mimicked her tone and appearance.

We both began to laugh as the atmosphere was toned down.

" Well I've actually bought you a new dress. I saw it in the window and knew straight away that this is your colour, what do you think?"

Emmett held this exquisite dress; the top was a beautiful plain pastel pink which cascaded into lace all the way to the bottom which trailed subtly to the floor with shiny silk.

" I think, that it's beautiful" I looked up feeling quite surprised at the gesture.

"I'll hang it above the door for now" Emmett said, placing it above the door.

"I meant to say, Emmett will you ask about at work to see if anyone knows of anyone who can fix that hole in the hedge?"

"Yeah of course I'll sort it, you just relax" he smiled.

As he walked out the door, I was left staring at the dress, I couldn't believe I had forgotten all about the book signing. Feels like I'm juggling a million and one things that I tend to forget what's going on around me. I let my feet slip to the end tilting my head back into the water. As I lay listening to the ripples of the water, a force restrained me and pushed my head until I was under water. I could feel a hand wrap around my throat, pushing me to the bottom of the tub. I struggled against the hand trying to lift myself above the water to breath yet the force was too strong to resist against. I began to feel light headed from lack of air, my body felt limp as though all the energy had been drained from within me.

Just as I felt it was all over, the force relieved from my throat leaving me able to push my way up. I gasped for breath and rubbed my eyes to see who was holding me down. There wasn't a person in sight, only the hair from my own head wrapped around my throat. I was convinced there was someone in here.

" What is it? , what happened? I could hear you shouting," Emmett came running in.

" There was , I felt..."were the only words that staggered out of my mouth.

"Felt what?" Emmett questioned in a perturbed manner.

"Nothing, I just slipped backwards just shocked me that's all" I exhaled still catching my breath.

" Okay. As long as you're okay?" he looked at me waiting for an answer yet still didn't look convinced that what I said was true.

I smiled and nodded gently as he left the room again. I waited for the footsteps to go into the distance before smacking my arms into the water splashing the whole side of the wall. I placed my chin into my chest where I let out a scream which turned into a cry of frustration. I was beginning to think I couldn't tell the difference between what's real and what's not. I can't tell if what everyone says is true. What if I am going mad?

Chapter 4

The air was cold that evening, the kind of cold were goosebumps tend to stick to your skin the whole time. I wasn't exactly dressed for the weather. We got to the outside of the book store. The windows were all lit up with Chloe's display of her books which were piled into pyramids, the store was packed with people all standing in little groups chatting amongst each other. I could feel my breath quicken with each step taken closer to the door, my flushed cheeks began to appear through my makeup. Emmett pushed the door open, the little bell on the top rang and with that the whole shop went silent. Everyone just started right at me. You could hear the mild sounds of chatter, the kind where you know they're talking about you. Chloe came strutting over to us breaking the silence in the room.

"I'm so glad you could both make it" her arms wrapped tightly around Emmett.

She never hugs me; in fact she becomes really awkward as though I'm a time bomb waiting to go off.

" And Bethany you're looking so well , good to see you out of the house." I didn't respond. I think my facial expression said exactly what I was thinking.

" My speech will start in 10 minutes so if you both want to get a drink and get settled and I'll see you both later on." She directed us to the refreshments table.

To my surprise I recognised the woman who was getting a coffee in front of us.

"Melanie." I peered around to see her face.

" Hiya are you alright? I didn't think I'd know anybody here" she said with a surprised tone.

"Yeah, Chloe's my sister-in-law," I responded.

"Oh right" Melanie said.

"So how did you hear about this, do you read?" I asked curiously.

" Yes, well to be honest I met Chloe a few weeks ago and she told me that she's a writer. She asked me and my husband Daniel to come along tonight, what a small world" she laughed weakly.

"Small world indeed" my face was half a smile whilst half a frown. "Could your husband not make it?" I asked with slight curiosity.

"Oh, erm, no me and my husband we're actually taking a break." The atmosphere turned into an awkward silence with everyone concentrating on what to say next.

"Oh I'm sorry , I shouldn't have asked."

 Melanie cut me short.

"No, no honestly it's fine, in fairness I was the one who said Chloe invited both of us, how were you supposed to know?"

Our conversation was cut short when Chloe's speech began, I could see her saying hello to Emmett nothing too deep just a simple greeting but I still don't understand why he spoke to her behind my back. The night consisted of small talk with that many different people, all the conversations started to sound the same, all I could think about was getting my shoes off and getting into bed.

I could see Emmett, Chloe and Melanie all stood talking amongst themselves I still couldn't help but feel like Emmett talks to Melanie about me more then I realise. I felt a bit awkward as though I was invisible or not worthy of talking to. I doubt that if I left now anyone would notice. I decided to walk over to see what they were all talking about but as soon as I got there the whole conversation stopped as if it was something they didn't want me to be a part of.

"Are you ready for the off?" I nodded with slightly uncomfortable feelings, thinking he didn't want me to be a part of this conversation.

"I'll see you tomorrow for our second session" Melanie reminded me of what I had to come up against tomorrow.

"Yeah, I'll see you tomorrow," was all I could say.

Emmett linked his arm to mine as we walked out the book store. The walk home was pretty quiet. I would have thought he would have at least mentioned something. We got upstairs to bed ,Emmett pulled off my heeled boots setting my feet free from being cramped in for hours. By the end of the night my dress had little creases on the bottom and yet as beautiful as it was I was happy to be getting into my pyjamas.

"So what were you, Chloe and Melanie talking about?" I knew if I didn't ask it would bug me all night.

"Oh Melanie was telling us about all the places she's been and how before she went into being a councillor, she wanted to be a journalist that's all." He looked at me like I was reading too much into it yet all night I couldn't sleep thinking he had just rehearsed what he was going to tell me.

Chapter 5

I woke up this morning to the sound of pounding rain, even the weather knew how I was feeling. The dark cold morning made me want to crawl under my duvet and never come out. I had a pretty scheduled day, today I was going back into work after a good few months off and then I am to go to my next counselling session later on in the evening. I looked above my wardrobe to see a creased shirt and a skirt with cotton threads spiralling down to the floor. And to top everything off I've only left myself half an hour to get ready and be out the door.

I managed to get myself ready with five minutes to spare which was needed due to me having to run to the car trying not to get wet. I hopped into the car and sorted out my smeared makeup and frizzy hair with drizzly rain still perched on top on my head. Luckly the dark misty air prevented anyone seeing me stressing to look presentable again, if I ever was in the first place. My flustered cheeks were quickly covered with powder and my hair was smoothed down. And then I began my journey to work.

I liked driving around this time of the morning, the eerie silence of quiet streets and the lights beaming from the cars. I took comfort in the fact that I'd be getting into work a little early today to ensure I'm all set up.

I arrived at the gates of the school where the playgrounds were near enough silent. I parked in my spot which hadn't been used in a while and that's when a slight bit of fear started to kick in. I wasn't so bothered about actually entering the school, just the thought of being at the front of a classroom with eyes staring at me as the sweat trickled down my forehead.

I slowly walked my way in, the good thing about coming in at this time is that there are no teenagers wondering in the corridors. After all how many kids would be in school earlier than they have to be? Although, this morning the whole place felt quieter than usual, I wasn't sure if it was just because I was more aware of everything and every feeling was heightened. I finally reached my classroom where everything was exactly the same as before. The last time I was in here was before we moved to the cottage and I remember spending so many weeks feeling on a high with the build-up of excitement.

"Bethany , is that you?"

"Helen, how are you?"

"Yeah, I'm not too bad thank you but more importantly, how have you been?"

"Yeah , you know I'm getting there"

"How do you feel about being back today?"

"Do you know what, I think this is exactly what I need to do, I need some normality back and this is where I need to be"

"Well I'm just glad to have you back, I have missed our little natters at break times"

"Me too, I haven't had a chance to talk to many people recently. That would require actually getting out and socialising." I smiled at my recognition of how I've been keeping myself to myself.

"How have the kids been?"

"Well they've had a supply teacher for a few weeks, so naturally winding her up was top of their list. But they've been fine , they're great kids and I'm sure they'll be thrilled to have you back today"

"I hope so"

"Well if you need me at all throughout the day , you know where I am"

"Thanks Helen"

I took a wonder around my classroom stroking my fingertips on all the tables. In a weird way I knew this was my classroom and everything was the same but it's like I haven't been in here for years and I can only remember a small amount of me ever being here as though it was all a memory or just in my imagination.

My silent thoughts and feelings where scuttled away by the sounds of shouting and loud talking as the room quickly began to get filled.

"Ah Mrs Pryon your back!"

"Nice to see you Millie" I happily replied back.

I took comfort in the fact that the kids were happy to see me as there's nothing scarier than trying your hardest to get it right not just for me, but for them too. My shoulders relaxed from my ears a bit more and my hands cooled down from their clammy touch.

"Good morning class, it's nice to see you all again! I'd like someone to tell me what you've been working on"

Lots of hands across the room shot up even I was taken back by the enthusiasm.

"I don't mind just shout out what you've been doing"

"Our learning objective has been to work on our creative writing and skills with our own ideas"

"Perfect , sounds like a fun task. Does anyone want to share their piece?. Doesn't have to be something you've written but I'd like to hear some ideas."

Many ideas were discussed for a good amount of time. As an English teacher I love to see children indulging and thriving in their writing and seeing how passionate they can be especially as today I'm teaching year seven so they're just starting out.

"I'm thinking that today you could all get into groups of four and discussing what you have so far, maybe even editing peoples work and giving them feedback, come up with your own idea and see if someone can help you."

Before I'd even finished, they'd all moved to the table that they wanted to sit at. I was grateful I came up with the idea when I did as I had no idea what I was going to do for a lesson today.

I wandered around the class listening quietly to all the brewing ideas each individual had, I eventually went and sat with a group to have a chat about their ideas.

"So, what ideas do we have on this table?"

"I like the idea about doing a romance story something in a nice setting in a pretty place."

"Okay so have you thought about characters , what are their personalities going to be like? How did these people meet? What's their back story? How do you want to start, will they meet straight away?" I felt happy to let my imagination run free with this too and be able to rebuild my creativity.

Emily looked really overwhelmed. "Sometimes I struggle with how to get my ideas onto paper."

"I'll tell you what, I'll get a big piece of A3 paper and we'll get mind mapping some ideas together"

I came back with an A3 sheet of paper and got thinking about ideas of my own to help them.

"So what ideas do we have?"

"I have an idea for a setting Mrs Pryon"

"Perfect, what's your idea Emily?"

"I was thinking about the countryside, maybe two people can meet in a small village"

"Yeah, and maybe they could live in some of those small houses"

"Oh yeah a cottage, that sounds perfect"

The chattering continued around me but I couldn't hear above the sound of my breath which had quickened once again. I could feel my body heating up as I grasp at the collar of my shirt for air. I place my hand on my chest trying to slow my breathing down. And then when I grew conscious at the fact that the whole table was watching me, I suddenly felt all eyes on me. I could see the children trying to get my attention asking me if I'm okay but it's like I physically couldn't answer as though my lips could make no sound. Eventually I realised that the whole class grew quieter and quieter, they could hear my panicked breathing until some of the children started shouting my name.

"Excuse me for a moment"

I moved as swiftly out of the classroom as I could and closed the door behind me. I let out gasps of sobs whilst scrunching my hair away from my sweaty forehead. I could hear the children shouting from one table to the other trying to work out what just happened and yet I didn't have any control over my own gasping and shouting.

"Mrs Pryon , is everything okay?" the headmaster came along the corridor looking a bit puzzled.

I shook my head with full force realising my breath hadn't slowed down enough for me to be able to speak.

"Can I help in any way?"

"I... I can't..." I couldn't finish my sentence and so I relaxed my head back against the wall in completely hopelessness.

"Right well come this way, I'll take you to my office. I'll just get Helen to cover your lesson."

I could hear the vague whispers of him talking to Helen but I couldn't fully hear what they were saying over my constant sniffling. My heels skipped with the sounds of clipping and clopping trying to walk as swiftly as I could before the bell rang and the corridors filled with people. We finally reached his office after what felt like an eternity and sat down on one of his comfy fluffy chairs, feeling defeated in every way. He sat down still in silence as though he was finding a way to begin what he wanted to say.

"Do you want to talk about what happened?" he finally blurted out.

"There isn't really much to tell" I declared.

"Is there anyone I need to speak to?"

I shook my head vigorously to ensure that no one is to blame but me, and that really was the truth. How was I ever going to get over this and why did I think I'd be able to come back this soon when even the mention of the word cottage sets me off.

"I think maybe you came back too soon, maybe some more time away could be the best option here?" His pitiful eyes stared back at me; everybody gives me those eyes these days.

"I just think I've got a lot to sort out, maybe I was too hard on myself for coming back in hast. But I cannot afford to be out of work, I've got to start paying my bills for my flat or we will be evicted in the next two weeks, another reason why I needed to come back" my voice began to tremble at the reality of being out of work , I could feel the panic rush through my head.

"Don't worry about that at all, I can put in a request for more sick leave and explain the circumstances. Leave it with me."

"Thank you"

"Don't thank me just go look after yourself Bethany and keep me informed on how you're doing won't you?"

"Yeah, I will do."

I near enough ran through the corridors bowing my head so far down I could barely see where I was going. I could hear people around me shouting and calling my name, I felt bad for being rude but I couldn't contain myself any longer.

I reached my car where I had been sat not even two hours ago. And yet for about another half an hour I just sat, staring, crying and scrubbing at my stinging, burning tired eyes. I wasn't sure if anything would be normal ever again. I couldn't help but wonder is this a nightmare which I will wake up from or is this now my life?

Chapter 6

I spent that night sitting in the room which has become so familiar to me sitting in the same chair I was in just 2 days ago.

" How you been doing Bethany?" Melanie started her long line of questions which felt a bit ambiguous.

"I erm I." I couldn't work out whether to tell her the truth or whether to tell her some overexaggerated lie about how great things have been. I chose to lie.

"Yeah, things have been fine." The fakest smile drew along my face.

"Is that the truth?" She responded with a slight raise to her eyebrows and a smile.

I knew she could tell I was lying even though I knew the biting of my lip and avoiding eye contact made that pretty obvious.

"Yes, it is," I didn't want to be asked loads more questions when it's difficult to answer the ones she has already asks me , there was no way I was going to make this any more difficult for myself.

"I'm not totally convinced if I'm honest"

"I just had a shitty day at work, I thought I was ready to go back and yet I couldn't even last the morning there. I feel so embarrassed and now I'm beginning to worry about what others around me must think of me."

"Theres nothing embarrassing about struggling Bethany. And to be honest I think that took great courage for you to try today and you did try your best, so don't be worried about needing more time, trauma isn't something which goes away overnight."

"But when will there be a time when I can be normal?" I pleaded for an answer.

"Stop putting pressure on yourself, don't worry about others around you. I'm not saying everyone understands what's going on with you and people might not always see the bigger picture, however once you take control and focus on yourself and not about what others might think , you'll find that your healing process will come naturally and you'll see that each day you'll feel that little bit better. Everything takes time Bethany so please don't worry." I could feel the realise of tension listening to Melanie's words , she always made me feel better and that whatever I am feeling is okay.

"I applaud your courage Bethany ; you never give up and yet you don't give yourself enough credit."

"I really appreciate that" and I really did too.

"Okay well on that note ,today I'd like us to discuss a further defined goal of how these sessions can help you cope with past trauma , is that okay?" This really was one of those rhetorical questions, I mean when have you ever heard someone actually say no or so much as disagree.

"Okay" the shallow sigh of breath left my dry clammed up throat.

"Trauma can affect people differently, you might find it can cause anxiety about things you wasn't anxious about before, you might feel tired from lack of sleep, whatever you are feeling or whatever you felt at the time I'd like us to collaborate on a plan of action and what you'd like to take out of these sessions. So today I don't want to ask you the questions I'd like you to tell me your first impact on your mental and emotional stability," She paused giving me a minute to process what she'd asked me to do.

" So last week you were talking about your first time actually seeing the cottage and how at the time you felt happy and excited so I'd like to know what was the contrast, when did those emotions change?" she explained.

It was barely evening when we arrived for the first time.

The cottage was so beautiful to the eye the defined colour of the cherry red door with matching window sills showing an elegant touch. Within a few minutes we'd hurriedly got out of the car and were standing at the door. The first push of the door simply took my breath away. The quaintness and tranquillity made the cottage feel a safe haven from the rest of the world.

"I'll get your suitcase out the car" I barely acknowledged what Emmett had said as my eyes wandered around the room, soaking up the warm, cosy feeling.

"Yeah, thanks babe" I responded automatically, as my eyes were still transfixed on the room. By the time we got all our belongings in the cottage the sky began to turn dark .

The first night we spent on mattresses and when I say mattresses, I mean ones we created made up of blankets and pillows. "Shit" Emmett went running through to the kitchen. "What is it?" I came in running behind him. He just stood there smiling whilst pulling out this burnt charcoaled pizza. We laid on our blankets peering over them to see the tv on the floor where all the wires twirled around the floorboards. "Mrs Pryon, can I offer you my best main meal of crispy cheese pizza?" We just burst into laughter at the sheer stupidity of burning something so simple. After eating our way through the best bits of the pizza the exhaustion had finally caught up with me, I could feel my eyes become heavy and before long I dozed off into a deep sleep , I was cozy with emmets arms and legs wrapped around me to keep me warm.

The next morning I was awoken by the light of dawn seeping into the room, the bright colours of deep rich tangerine- orange spurt through the white laced netting of the curtains. The twists of sun rays shone in ripples on the laminate flooring making their own patterns. Through my small yet heavy breaths I inhaled the cold crisp air that fogged around me and extended

35

throughout the air. I didn't realise how cold it had become overnight. I stood up on my rested feet where my limbs extended to a forceful stretch.

It was already late morning; Emmett had already left for work so I found myself pottering about the house beginning to unpack. I began to get a chill as the light around me dimmed from the thick grey blanket unfolding across the sky. In search of my long-knitted cardigan that kept the warmth close to my skin, I couldn't help but be alarmed by a slight bit of movement outside. I couldn't be sure but it looked like somebody was standing to the side of my window. Pulling my cardigan over my chest wrapping my arms close to me I found the closest shoes to me and let my curiosity take me further.

I opened the door to nothing but the air, not even the air felt disturbed, by this point I assumed I had imagined the whole scenario.

"Hello there."

A gasp flew out of my mouth as my body turned so quickly, my hair wiped right across my face.

"Sorry I did knock I didn't think there was anyone in." In front of me was a man with a beautiful gleaming smile, he was tall and broad yet he had a gentleness about him kind of like a teddy bear.

"What can I help you with?" I asked actually feeling a bit shy.

"Oh right sorry, I was the gardener for the person who lived here before and I was just coming to enquire if you needed me to do the gardening for you?" He replied.

"Oh right well I'll be honest I didn't know there even was a gardener so I haven't had a chance to check with my husband but I can't see there being an issue, actually I was just saying to my husband briefly yesterday that there's a hole in the hedge at the back , big enough that someone could see in, so at some point could you take a look at that?" I queried.

"I can take a look now ; I've got a bit of spare time" he implied.

"That would be perfect thank you, come inside." I stepped back to let him through.

"I'll just get my tools out the van, I won't be a minute" That beautiful, warm smile still across his face.

"No worries, oh what's your name by the way?"

"Dan , and you are?"

"Bethany but my friends call me Beth"

"Nice to meet you Beth, I'll be in in a minute" he jogged up to his van which was parked at the top of the road. I was impressed by his confidence but I could tell under his humorous side he had beautiful, kind qualities.

Patiently waiting for Dan to come through to the garden I realise I never noticed how beautiful the scenery was.

The endless ray of flowerpots upon crisp cut grass. Even on a grey, foggy day such as this the garden felt warm, vibrant with endless amounts of colour.

"Sorry for the wait, where abouts is the hole?" he asked.

"Just at the back of the hedge here," I directed him.

For at least 10 minutes Dan pushed, progged , moved and scratched at this hole before looking at me with great curiosity.

"Was this already here before you moved in?" He was still looking at the hole.

"Erm, well it was there when I came out last night before we went to bed so I just assumed wildlife had scratched their way in looking for food or shelter, why is there something wrong?"

"Not necessarily something wrong but I personally don't think this was wildlife , this looks like it's actually been cut through by a person"

I wasn't really sure of what he was subtly trying to imply.

"I won't beat around the bush but is there any chance someone would have tried to get in?" he asked whilst still waying up the possibilities.

"What on earth for?"

" I don't want to alarm you but I think it would be best to get security cameras just as a precaution. However in the meantime, I've got a security light in the back of my van which you can have so it can alert you, if there is a person trying to get in while your asleep you'll know as the light will come on. then you might find out who's trying to sleep in your garden" his tenderness radiated from his laugh, which I might add was very infections.

"Can I get you a tea or coffee before you go?"

"Yeah, coffee would be great, milk and two sugars." We went through and sat in the living room.

A whole hour had already ticked by, the sky had folded over into quite a dark evening and yet the conversation wasn't drawing to a close.

"Do you live locally or....?"

"Yes, yes, I do. I actually live up the road , well I used to live with my wife but we split a few months ago" I couldn't tell how he felt about his current situation.

"Oh I'm sorry to hear that"

"Oh no that's fine I'm getting through it." He let out a small smile I could tell that underneath he was still a bit hurt.

"Can I get you another cup?" I offered, trying to change the atmosphere.

" No, I better be getting home , thank you for the coffee though"

Just then Emmitt stood on the right side of the doorway.

"Who's this?" he eventually asked after a cold hard stare at Dan.

"Oh , this is Dan"

" Nice to meet you mate." Dan held out his hand whilst Emmett reluctantly waited to shake it.

"He's a gardener and noticed this place was occupied again and wanted to know if we needed help with the garden so I thought I'd ask him to sort the hole out in the hedge"

"And yet it's still not sorted" Emmett snapped.

"Well no but for the time being he's giving us a security light"

Emmett grunted whilst walking away , to be honest I had no idea why he had given Dan such a cold shoulder. Though it did cross my mind that men will be men defending their territory even when there is no threat.

"I'll see you to the door Dan"

Walking through to the door my eyes were narrowed by staring right at Emmett

" I can come back tomorrow to put the light up if you like"

Emmett shot through to the door not giving me a chance to answer.

"Well I can put it up tomorrow , I don't have work." His sharp tone snapped back in again.

"Okay , well I'll just go get it then" Dan said before leaving the door.

"What's wrong with you?"

"What do you mean?"

"Why did you snap so much at Dan? he's doing us a favour" I didn't want to argue with him yet I did feel angry at the situation.

"I know , I know I wish you would have told me he was coming. I'm tired that's all, it's been a long day" he replied letting out an exaggerated sigh.

I felt bad but I was still annoyed enough to not give a dignified answer, he was acting as though I knew Dan was coming.

"Here you go one security light"

"Thank you," I said, smiling back.

I had now realised that the last part of this conversation I was never actually talking to Melanie I was just reminiscing about what had happened. I worried about talking to Melanie about Emmett even though that happened ages ago I didn't want any conflict if they ever spoke again.

However I also noticed that Melanie seemed a little on edge as though something I had said seemed to bother her. Her hands seemed kind of clammy and I think I could even see a line of sweat fall down the side of her head.

Our session was cut short when her phone rang which I think seemed a bit suspicious considering it looked like she was just messaging on her phone only minutes before. She said we'd pick the conversation up next week which also got me thinking about what could have been getting her so worked up. I didn't even notice when she started to get worked up due to my thinking process of what I was telling her and my hard concentration of remembering what happened that night in the cottage. Usually our sessions actually finished a bit late, so why was today so different? Maybe I was paranoid and this was nothing to do with anything I said.

Chapter 7

Upon my fairly quick leave from my session I couldn't tell what had even happened within the last ten minutes, maybe I was that engrossed in what I was thinking I became unaware of my surroundings. However I definitely must have been in there for nearly an hour. I could tell by the change of darkness to the clouds outside, there wasn't that mid-evening bloom of brightness that there was when I went in.

Glancing through the glass of the reception pacing over to the revolving doors I saw a face which I was fairly certain that I recognised, he was tall, I would definitely say no shorter than 6 foot he wore a jacket of a dark brown along with matching dark trainers. The feature that stood out the most was the beautiful smile he wore and that's when I knew who he was.

"Dan?" I said whilst not even getting fully out of the door.

"Beth , hi , how are you?" his voice travelled in a mellow tone.

"Yeah, I'm not too bad thank you, how are you?"

"Yeah, I'm good. Did you have an appointment?"

I began to feel a slight bit of embarrassment , I don't know what it is but telling someone you're having counselling can feel like a hard thing to say.

"Yeah" I replied with only a slight bit of noise which fell out of my mouth.

"Sounds like a touchy subject, I was just going to get a coffee from town. Would you like to join me?"

The sound of normality and having a conversation with someone who isn't going to judge me sounded just perfect at this moment.

"I would love that." I sighed out with relief of having a chat with a friendly face.

"I've just got to run these papers into someone inside, I shalt be a moment"

He was no sooner in and out of the reception before we took a slow walk to the corner coffee shop.

" So how have you been keeping?" He broke the ice with such an ordinary question but how could I tell him the truth that I was feeling anything but ordinary or normal at the moment?

" Yeah , well to be honest I don't know how to answer that, it's fair to say that it's been a bit of a roller-coaster over this month"

" Well I'll be honest I was a little shocked when I saw someone else had moved into the cottage , you guys weren't exactly in there for long."

"No, I know, that's mainly my fault."

His big stunned eyes were now staring back at me just waiting for me to tell him the story. Little did he know what he was letting himself in for. Before beginning at the start we managed to get to the coffee shop where I could at least sit down.

"What would you like? I'll get these"

I was a little taken back by his kindness and warmth.

"Oh erm, are you sure?" My voice was high pitched with surprise.

"Yes of course I am"

"I'll have a flat white then please , thank you"

The queue was nearly stretched out of the door meaning I had time to get myself together before he came back and asked me the inevitable questions.

"Here you go, so you were saying?"

"So from the last time I saw you and you gave me the security light , I'll be honest before you said anything I didn't even think anything of the hole but then every time I saw the light go off, I got disturbed by my paranoia" I scarcely laughed at my own naivety.

"Oh gosh I'm sorry I never meant to scare you I was just..."

"No honestly, I'm so glad you said what you did because otherwise I wouldn't have noticed this at all. Emmett put the light up the next morning perfecting the place and angle for a good half an hour before being satisfied but it made me feel better knowing that we would be aware of any intruders, well so I thought anyway"

"It wasn't faulty or anything was it?" his face turned a slightly pale shade.

"No not at all if anything I wouldn't of notice what would come next if it wasn't for the light. I was in bed; we'd finally got our bed up in our bedroom, a relief from sleeping on the floor in the living room or so I thought it would be but I felt a bit restless and spent most the night tossing and turning. I gave up trying to sleep and ended up looking out at the beautiful night sky through the kitchen window.

The moon was full and bright so I hadn't realised that the security light was on until I saw a dark figure had approached the garden. I woke Emmett up and asked him to go out and see but the person had vanished into the night, so as you can imagine that was my first initial scare. From then on, I don't think I have had one night sleep without being woken by every gust of wind to every leaf rustling.

"Wow I'm so sorry you had to go through that , did you find out who it was?"

46

"No, luckily it was just the one time. I think that you giving me the security light when you did was my protector that night so I'll be honest I should be the one paying for the coffee not you."

His cheeks had a haze of red through his freckles as his eyes wandered down to his spoon where he was swirling the froth of his coffee around the mug.

"My turn. What were you doing outside Merkley house? I assume it wasn't a councillor you were expecting to see."

"No, I was actually dropping off my divorce papers"

We both went quiet due to the fact that I hadn't replied to his comment not really knowing how to.

"My wife , she works there and I don't see her anywhere else but I know where she works so it was just the easiest thing to do"

"Oh right, yeah you said you were getting a divorce the last time I saw you ; I'm surprised you haven't already started the procedure of divorce."

"I'll be honest Melanie, she's not the easiest to arrange this kind of thing with."

The expression on my face said all the possible things I was thinking, I couldn't believe I'd been sitting with my councillors ex-husband the whole time and little did I know that I had actually been in the middle of something I didn't even know anything about.

"Melanie, you say?"

"Yeah, do you know her?" His tone rose as he looked at me with suspicion.

"Well as a matter of fact, yes, she's, my councillor!" I said feeling a bit uncomfortable.

"Oh, I see"

Neither of us said a word , just the sound of heavy breathing and heavy slurps highlighted in an awkward silence.

Eventually we both broke the silence by speaking both at once

"Sorry you go first" I smiled.

"I was just going to ask how long have you been seeing Melanie?"

" I've only just had my second session, so I only started this week"

"Oh right I thought it would have been longer. What were you going to say?"

"I was just going to ask if you don't mind me doing so , why are you and Melanie getting a divorce?"

" Well it just wasn't working ; she'd be working late most nights so we weren't actually seeing much of each other so I guess you could say we just drifted."

"Yeah, I get that"

"So that's why I was dropping off the papers because as I said I don't see her anywhere else."

I nodded with a smile.

" As much as I could sit here and talk all day I better be getting back as I've got a few houses to get to before night draws."

"That's okay it was nice to see you again, I'm sure I'll see you about"

"Oh yeah definitely" he replied adamantly.

" And as for my counselling sessions they're quite straight to the point so I shan't be saying any more than that." I didn't have to say any more than that as Dan knew exactly what I was talking about.

"Thank you, Beth, I really appreciate that. You take care"

" And you." We walked in our separate directions yet as I took the walk-through town, I couldn't help but wonder if there was more to the story then Dan was letting off.

Chapter 8

The next day I achieved nothing, which is pretty standard. I was still taking in what I was told last night which I think is half the reason I'm tired today, considering I was laid in bed all night overthinking how I was caught in between a divorce. All morning I caught up on series I've wanted to binge for ages, now I have no job to go to , this is now my typical day.

I must have slept the whole afternoon, I fell asleep to the late morning haze of the sun, which at the time ,still lingered through the clouds, yet the crepuscular rays of sun gave a warmth in the air. But by this time the sky's atmosphere became quiet and settled only being lit up by the teeming stars. I stood gazing in ore upon the stars and moonlit sky. It began to occur to me that the time the sky tells must also be that Emmett should have been home quite a bit before now.

Still partially in my sleep inertia phase of heavy eyelids and being slightly disoriented I reached over to my phone where no notifications had been left on my screen. It was strange of Emmett to be home late but even more so for him not to have rang or so much as left a message.

The time read eight forty- two. Emmett usually reaches home at the time of five just in time for dinner which has not been prepared due to me having been in a deep sleep brought on by exhaustion. My phone rang out yet there was no answer from his end of the phone, I could feel the panic begin to race through my veins as the questions grew louder and louder in my thoughts. What if something happened? what if he couldn't get to his phone?

It had been 20 minutes since I had bombarded Emmett's phone with calls and messages simply asking if he could at least let me know what's going on, yet still no reply. Something to do was better than sitting around so I decided to take on the job of doing all the small things that needed to be done around the house. I stood leant against the sink as the fast stream of water filled the bowl splashing the worktops.

My eyes were so fixated on the water that the bowl began to overflow. I knew I couldn't concentrate on anything else. In haste I grabbed my car keys and leapt to the door. On the other side stood Emmett who had a rather nervous face and rightly so.

"Not even a message, nothing at all!" I bellowed.

"I know , I know I'm sorry" he tiptoed into the house trailing behind me to the kitchen.

"Where have you been?"

"I had some work to finish up and I didn't want to leave it until the morning"

"What for three hours? "I paused to check my watch to be exact.

"There was a backlog of phone calls and writing up records that just needed to be completed"

"Right, and you couldn't message to tell me that?"

"Well yes I could have done but to be honest Beth I didn't realise I still had a curfew"

"It's not about that Emmett , when you come home the same time every night, I obviously expect you to be home at that time"

"I would have messaged but I wanted to get finished so I didn't end up sitting there all night, that's all"

"I'm going upstairs to run the bath; I didn't do any dinner because I didn't know what time you were going to be home." my voice returned to a calmer collective mood.

"That's fine, I'll sort something "he replied.

By the time I trudged up the stairs I just lay on bed too exhausted to move so much as a finger. It wasn't that I was tired I just had no energy in me to move.

Emmett finally came upstairs to where I was still laid at the bottom of the bed .

"Are you tired?"

"No" I sharply reply.

"So is there a reason you're laid at the bottom of the bed?"

I could feel the tears welling up in the corner of my eyes.

"That's just it, I'm not tired. I've just had a good four hours sleep on the sofa yet I have no energy to do anything. I don't go anywhere; see anyone. I'm not in work now I've been advised to take more time off and even when I was for a while they cut back on my hours so I was barely in anymore. And even when I was in, I could tell they were all talking about me. After my last break down I'm not sure if I'll ever be able to go back in again. I go to counselling, come home and just sit there all day. I've got no one to talk to and I'm fed up of feeling useless." I obviously didn't realise myself how much I needed to ramble and express how I felt.

"You can talk to me"

Emmett went to come in for a cuddle but I couldn't bear the thought of being held at the moment, I would probably never stop crying.

"No Emmett I can't , you didn't even tell me you were going to be home late so it's not like I could have gone anywhere or done anything anyway."

"I know but I'm home now and I've said I'm sorry , I don't know what else you expect from me."

"I was just worried that's all."

" I know and I am sorry."

I leant in a bit closer as he sat perched on the end of the bed waiting for me to accept that hug.

"Come here , look why don't you go out tomorrow and do something it might help with how you are feeling?"

"Well I've decided ,I'm going to message Poppy and see if she wants to meet up, I just want to see a friendly face and have a normal conversation."

"Oh , right"

"I know you're not a fan of each other but she's my best friend Emmett and I could do with a little support from her right now"

"Okay, whatever you need"

"Thank you, I'll message her now"

I already felt a bit better at the ping of my phone with a message from Poppy who was well up for a catch up.

"I've known poppy since we were at school Emmett, we've always been best friends"

"Well ,when has she been there for you recently?"

"That's not fair, we have different lives now compared to seeing each other every day at school and I don't expect her to check in on me constantly."

I used to look up to poppy when we were younger, I was always the tag along in her story , she was always the main character. But I liked it that way as I could learn so much from her. We had very different upbringings; her parents had their own business so were never around at home much whilst my parents gave me quite a sheltered life so by the time I got to secondary school Poppy had so much to teach me and I had so much to learn. She taught me how to have a fashion sense , skirts that showed enough bum cheek so you could get away with walking down the street without getting a bollocking from your neighbours but still being able to catch the eyes of the gorgeous boys who lived at the end of the street. She taught me how to kiss with tongues in an attractive way as opposed looking like two puppies slobbering all over each other and most importantly she taught me how to love myself and always had a way of making me feel like the most important person. I couldn't wait to see her as I miss the days we would spent hours together.

"Right well I'm off to run that bath, and tomorrow if she ends up coming back here you will be nice won't you or at least be civilised to each other for your sake?"

"Of course I will"

"Good. I don't even know why you both don't get along" I smiled whilst saying that sentence as I left the room but as I did, I only heard a small amount of what Emmett said before it all became mumbled.

" I haven't the slightest idea..."

Chapter 9

I had arrived at the coffee shop a little earlier than we had said we'd meet up. It gave me time to have a moment of peace , to be sat with my own thoughts. I was so happy to be having a conversation with someone where I don't have to think about everything I say.

"Hello stranger" came from the voice I knew only so well.

I leapt from my chair and threw my arms around her.

"Oh look you've started without me" Poppy said whilst looking at my very full cold coffee.

" No I've been here for a while"

"Beth is actually early for something ; something must be up . Let me get a drink and you can tell me all about everything."

Poppy never failed to make me laugh. She is very strong minded with a lot of confidence which is something I always lacked greatly in.

"So how you been doing my lovely? I know it's been a rough couple of months"

" It's all just come at me so quick like a slap right slap in the face, I feel as though since moving back to the city I live the same day every day."

"Are you getting the support you need?" she asked, waiting for an honest answer.

"Well I've started counselling; I've only had a few sessions so far but I know that by the time my next sessions comes to call I need to just get it all off my chest"

"I think that will help you massively , I know it's not easy for you but letting other people help won't be the be all and end all."

" I know"

" And what about at home are you getting the support there?" she sheepishly picked up her coffee and touched it to her lips.

"From Emmett?" I said, raising my eyebrow.

"Yep, you know what I'm talking about"

"If I'm being completely honest, we were arguing over everything and nothing at the moment and I kept thinking it was me because of me struggling but I don't know if there's more to it."

"Well, have you spoken to him?"

"Not about that but we spoke about how I need to start getting out the house a bit more so maybe he's starting to realise and I'll get more support."

"Good luck with that" she had that same look as though she was waiting for me to react.

"Look, I know you don't like him…"

"I just don't like how he talks to you; I actually think he's kind of shady."

"He is not shady Poppy , honestly."

"Okay well I just think he's wrong for you, I'm just saying this as a friend."

"He's had a lot on his plate at the moment and I know it's not easy when your wife is struggling."

"But surely he should be there for you all the more."

"I know you mean well but can we change the subject." I began to feel uncomfortable but not because of what she said but I have been thinking a lot about why he's been so snappy.

"So how do you find being back at your flat?"

"It's a weird feeling , we spent so much time packing up our stuff thinking we were moving out to then being in exactly the same place."

" I can't imagine how difficult things have been for you and I'm really sorry I haven't been in contact with you that much."

"No please , it was actually easier to just have my own company for a while. So what's been going on with you?"

"Well there is something I do actually want to talk to you about."

I felt the need to stretch my back up and raise my head to her attention.

"When you left for the countryside, I started talking to this guy. He added me on Facebook and from there we just got chatting. And then he started asking me out on dates and something between us just clicked."

"Awh Poppy I'm so happy for you , so how many dates have you been on with him."

"We've actually been seeing each other for a year now , and this is the bit I want to tell you. The other day he asked me to marry him !"

" No way " the disbelief stood out in my voice from my quick response. She showed me this gorgeous glistening ring with a white, crystal diamond

By this point everyone in the shop was staring at our table from where screeches and shrikes of happiness overpowered the room.

"Oh Poppy, this is amazing news."

"I know I'm so excited it's finally happening."

I passed her a tissue as the mascara fell onto her cheek.

"When's the date of the wedding?"

"Oh, we're not sure yet I think we're still getting used to saying the word fiancé."

"I bet"

"You never know you might find someone at my wedding to marry."

"Poppy! I'm fully committed to my marriage with Emmett"

"I'm only joking," she said whilst jokily nudging me.

" Actually I forgot to say , I have a new friend." I said whilst smiling avoiding eye contact.

"Oh really , and who might this friend be"

"He's a very nice ,sophisticated man who I can easily talk to ."

"Oh this friend is a he , how very interesting."

"It's not like that" I laughed.

"What does he look like?"

"He's tall, has a really nice smile and he really listens to everything and anything I want to talk about."

"Sounds like the perfect match" she implied

"Again it's not like that"

"Oh, but you've definitely thought about it," she murmured.

"No , no we actually met because he was our gardener at the cottage," I was cut off by Poppy making sounds from being engrossed in my storytelling.

"Hmmm" she drew in closer.

"And then I saw him again and he asked me to go for a coffee, but only for a chat."

"Sounds like he might have thought otherwise."

"That's where you're wrong , his ex-wife is actually my councillor so as you can imagine that put a spanner in the works"

"So he's divorced?" she implied again.

"Poppy, take this seriously , there is nothing going on there," my face became a bit more serious this time .

"I am happy with Emmett , we're just in a bit of a bumpy phase," I reassured her.

"Okay , fine" she carried on with her wandering eyes and giggly smile.

We spent the whole afternoon girly gossiping and giggling our way through the day. I didn't want the day to end. It felt like everything had gone back to normal and to be honest I didn't want to go home.

"You know, I've really missed you" Poppy linked her arm around mine, snuggling into my side as we walked down the avenue.

"I've missed you more"

"I've missed you the most"

I always felt safe around Poppy , she always had my back.

"Oh my gosh, did I tell you I saw Mrs Smith in Tk Maxx the other day"

"No way did she recognise you?"

"Of course she did , I just wanted to walk in front of her and pull my skirt down and say 'is that knee length enough'" she said whilst bursting into laughter whist re-enacting her story.

"When were we ever not in trouble?" I said trying to reflect on many times we would mess about together.

"We were always in trouble"

"I blame you; I think you were a bad influence"

"Me? oh please, you always had it in you. I just brought out your bad bitch side"

"My parents always dreaded me coming home when I'd been with you, waiting me to walk through the door pissed up and stumbling through the door"

"At least your parents had an opinion , my parents were never around to see or know anything about me."

I always felt sorry for Poppy, even though I was pretty babied for my whole life I couldn't never imagine not being close to my parents and family.

"Well you know , I remember one night my parents saying 'Poppy will bring out the best in you, and even though you can make some questionable choices when your with her, she always has your back and it's hard to find a friend who will guide you and look out for you the way she does'"

"You never told me that"

"Yeah I promise you, they said that the night after I came home from the leavers party. Then we went off to different colleges and kind of drifted our own ways and I remember thinking so clearly, what if you find other friends and don't need me anymore, how can I ever not have my Poppy to guide me?" I was still smiling at how naive I was then.

"What's wrong?" I noticed that she slightly squinted with water glossing over her eyes.

"No one has ever made me feel the way you have and as much as you thought you hid behind me , you never needed me , for anything I was the one who wanted you all to myself. I remember when I went off to college I sat at my desk panicking that my other half wasn't sat here with me because she was such a clever clogs that she went off to learn and study English. And that terrified me so much Bethany." By this point we stood face to face right in the middle of the Highgate both nearly in tears.

"And that's why I wanted to ask you; will you be my maid of honour?"

"You want me?"

"Are you joking? Of course I do , if you're not there stood beside me I don't think I'd be able to get married as the most important person to me wouldn't be there" she grabbed hold of both my hands squeezing them with anticipation of what I will say.

"Of course I will, it will be my honour!" I felt a warm tingling inside my stomach , the feeling of excitement something I had longed to feel. And the feeling of having purpose again.

"I'm so happy because we have got some serious shopping to do, I've got to get off today because I'm meeting Henry for dinner but I'll message you and we'll get started next week, how does that sound?"

"That sounds incredible, but just one more thing, when will I get to meet Henry because I need to see if he's perfect enough for my girl." I questioned with my bad bitch face on, I'd forgotten what that felt like to have fun like the giggly ,girly school girls we used to be.

"Well why don't me and Henry and you and Emmett go out for dinner at the weekend like a cute double date? it'll be nice for you all to get to know each other before the big day."

"I'd love that , I'll talk to Emmett tonight"

"Well that's sorted then , let me know what he says"

"I will do"

"Right I better get off babes but definitely message me later, love you lots"

"I love you more"

Just as I thought she'd already walked off long and far enough to not hear anything I was saying , I heard a clear and confident shout.

"I love you the most."

Chapter 10

The night fell dark in the city, it wasn't particularly late but the drizzle of rain had drawn the day to night faster. The large pillows of thick grey wandered through to the city from which the rain broke through the clouds starting in small patches. The city's atmosphere was overwhelmed with people rushing in from the cold , getting into cars or taxis which filled up the spaces on the cluttered road.

And even though the city was alive, the sound of the harmonic rain patting against my window left me in a peaceful sleep. The constant euphonious sound of the rain clashing to my window was the perfect lullaby to doze off to.

I was fairly certain I'd have a good night's sleep tonight due to how relaxed I was when I drifted off. I couldn't tell if I was thinking this or if I was having another episode of a hypnopompic state. Although normally I can tell when I have woken up as my dreams go off into a distance and become a memory.

I could see the colour red flickering through my visions and as the colour expanded, I could see the door to the cottage right before my eyes. I stood as though I was there. The door swung open and on the porch was the man, the man who was there that night.

My feet ran as fast as they would, they took me back through the woods that were filled with miles and miles of endless trees. I came to a standstill, not by choice but my feet wouldn't take me any further. I looked up to see that I was in the spot where my feet were pulled beneath me. This time I didn't scream because I could actually stand on my feet.

I was opposite a man who only appeared to wear black, he had his hands clenched in a tight fist. His boots were of a big size and his footprints could be seen behind him. Just as I was about to scream, he came running at me at lightning speed. My eyes opened, but only to the sight of my bedroom ceiling. I could now tell the night had come upon us; the city was lit up by the rows of brightly coloured lights. The rain was still pouring from the clouds, but now the sound of wispy rain had been transformed to a heavy downpour.

It was still relaxing enough to listen to and watch. I tried not to wake myself up completely, I shuffled my way into the duvet just for a small amount of comfort. But pulling up the duvet , I realised that I didn't have to haul it onto me like I usually do. I sharply rolled to my other side to see what I had expected. Emmett wasn't laid next to me, yet I was certain that he came to bed.

I pierced my lips together and listened carefully to the muffled voice that I could hear coming from the next room. I arose out of my bed to meet with the creaking floorboards where the sounds were covered up by the downpour outside. The murmured whispers turned to frustrated shouting which echoed all the way down the hall. Each step closer I took I couldn't decide whether I should be scared or if I'd got so used to expecting to be scared. I turned the corner of the kitchen which is where I saw Emmett arguing on the phone.

" I don't care anymore I want it done"

A silence in the room emerged as the person on the receiving end of the phone was talking I assumed.

"Look, we don't have much time left to finish this , I want you to do your part and I'll do mine. Then this will all be over"

My vision began to disfigure but this time blinking couldn't even adjust my eyes. My head went light headed and hazy. My breathing became laboured , the centre of my palms came to a sweat. This wasn't like my usual panic attacks; I couldn't control this. Emmett looked over to my direction where he hastily put down the phone. By this point I was clutching to my chest which felt as though it couldn't get any tighter.

 Just as I could see the shadow of Emmett approaching me , my chest loosed along with my uptight limbs. But I could tell I was falling as I could no longer feel the wall against my back. Floating in the air, I could see the dark figures of a man. I might have had a hazy vision but before I hit the floor, I could tell I was still conscious. It was him; he was back.

Chapter 11

Bethany, Bethany, can you hear me?"

"Where ,w-where"

"You're in the hospital , you collapsed at home, can you remember?" the nurse queried.

"B-but that man , h-he was there"

"What man?"

"T-the one who was in my house" I said whilst trying to catch my breath.

"Do you mean your husband?, your husband said he'd just got in the door when he found you passed out on the floor."

I wasn't conscious enough to say what I wanted to but then again, I wasn't sure what I did want to say. I distinctly remember Emmett on the phone , why would he lie? Or if I didn't, why would my visions take me to such a thought?

"We'd like to keep you here under observation today, your husband rang to say he'd arranged for your counselling appointment to be here today. He thinks you need to talk to someone."

I blinked my eyelids in a response to her comment so she knew I had heard what she had said.

"Try to get some rest this morning , you should see a remarked improvement this afternoon."

She placed a gentle hand on my shoulder before leaving the room.

I spent my whole morning dozing in and out of sleep whilst watching the nurse come in and out of my room. Sleeping did make me feel better although I can't say it helped with the memories of what actually happened. As I was just about to doze off to sleep, a cold gust of wind passed through to my bed. Melanie had just walked through the door.

"Hello Bethany," Melanie's voice beckoned from the doorway.

Silence fell through the room ; you could hear each footstep draw louder and closer to the chair which sat beside me.

"How are you feeling?"

"Well besides lying in a hospital bed with no memory of how or what got me here , yeah fine"

She just smiled sarcastically as though she was prepared for my mood of the day.

"I think today it's important that whatever you feel is necessary to get off your chest we will discuss, would that be okay for you ?"

"Yes, I see no problem with that"

"Just before we begin , might I ask what you remember from last night?"

"I must admit not a lot, before I could tell what was going on , my mind went blank."

I drew my eyes away from Melanie , I did not want to say what I hoped I hadn't seen if I was honest.

"Beth, in order for me to help you I need you to speak freely with honesty."

"Your saying to trust you"

"Precisely, I can't help with your problems if I don't know what they are. This is a safe space to speak freely "

My breath felt long as my shoulders dropped from besides my ears.

" I need to understand how you are feeling Beth so I can help you make changes , some issues you may think are small compared to the deeper issues but you might find that slowly pacing through and eliminating each little problem can help you open up not only to me but yourself."

"What do you mean opening up to myself?"

"well, have you actually thought about what triggers your panic attacks, or how you feel before one comes on?"

"I suppose mainly when I feel threatened or uncomfortable"

"Okay and when do you mainly feel these feelings?"

"I don't know really; I suppose when I'm on my own"

"That's really good that you've been able to recognise that and maybe going forward something good to do might be to track these thoughts and feelings and see where the patterns lie"

"Yeah, I suppose"

"Well when did these feelings first start to be recognizable to you?"

"I first started to have these feelings our last week of staying in the cottage , the time I felt most vulnerable"

"I know this has been a massive difficulty for you to speak about what happened in the cottage as you barely bring up the topic until I ask so that indicates to me that this might be the stem of the problems here"

My shoulders began to tense back up to my ears which were red hot.

"I think the time has come to tell me what happened at the cottage, don't you think?"

I took my last sigh of relief before looking straight in Melanie's eyes and let the words begin to roll off my tongue.

Chapter 12

Thursday 18th June 2018 21:54

The sound of the heavy footsteps awoke me from my sleep , not fully awake but enough to ponder on what the noise could be. There was someone inside the cottage, I was fairly certain. I lay there feeling uneasy , slightly trembling at the thought of walking down the stairs to find someone actually down there. The rhythmic thud echoed louder and louder until I was convinced they were actually below the bed. My eyes flickered side to side listening, waiting to hear the next moves.

The footsteps started up again but this time the sound of the floor was different , the floor wasn't heavy but hollower like the sound of tiptoeing slowly up the stairs. Even though I could feel the heart palpitations reflecting on my heavy breathing, I could not lay there pondering anymore. I swung my legs off the bed , I pulled my closest dressing gown from above the door and stood on the other side of the wall, waiting for the right time for me to move.

Every beat of my heart a footstep closer up the stairs was taken, until they stopped. I still stood waiting for them to start up again but they didn't, my adrenaline forced me to the top of the stairs where I was convinced,

I would be facing eyes to eyes with what could potentially be the last face I ever saw.

The stairs were as empty as the rest of the house, not even the ruffle of the carpet from prints of shoes could be seen. I quickly came to a swift walk to reach downstairs which led to a gust of wind coming from an open door, the only clue to there ever being someone here.

I slammed the door with full force trying to wake up Emmett who had slept through the whole entire thing. With one last skim of the rooms I took myself back to bed, where I wondered if I'd been all along.

"What was that massive bang?" Emmett stood at the top of the stairs, alarmed.

"Didn't you hear?"

"Hear what?"

"There was someone in here , could you not hear the footsteps coming up the stairs?"

"Did you see who it was?" Emmett came bounding down the stairs, nearly knocking me off them.

"No they left before I got to them but the door was wide open when I got down here"

"Go back to bed and I'll get someone to change the locks tomorrow just in case there was a spare key which someone has"

I laid on top of the bed staring at all the patterns on the ceiling , my eyes frozen wide but still felt heavy as though it were an effort to move them.

The patterns began to get smaller and smaller as my wide eyes drew smaller and smaller until the darkness of sleep was all I could see.

Friday 19th June 2018 07:45

I woke in the exact same position as I fell asleep as though the fear had frozen me still. Emmett had left for work already and even though the night had turned to day I still could not help but feel uncomfortable by the company of myself and being all alone. I felt like this majority of the morning as I pottered around, unpacking to ease my mind.

Emmett had left a note on the side to say he'd arranged for someone to change the locks today; I was quite grateful to be having the company if I was honest. I stood waiting at the window, just looking out to the far land which covered the whole area, which got me thinking about who would know how to get here, could it be someone who lived local?

A strong knock from the door echoed through the back room where I was standing.

I opened the front door, just wide enough to see the face of who was on the other side.

"Hello?" my voice sounded unsteady.

"Hello I'm Leon" he stated as though I was supposed to know who he was.

"Leon?" I held on hand on the door for comfort of being able to close the door if I felt threatened.

"I'm here to change the locks on the doors" he reassured.

"Oh right , come in" I let my hand relax against the door to accept him coming in.

I listened to him rambling all afternoon, he seemed like a lovely bloke but all I could hear was the fuzziness of everything around me as I stood in a daydream. Just as I shut my eyes with a strong awakening blink, the light shone along the cold shiny tiles as my eye caught the glimpse of something dusted along the floor.

The mark was a dusted white , like the kind when you've walked through gravel or the stones from a driveway. I couldn't be sure if it was his or not but I wasn't convinced as this was nowhere near where he was working.

My ears were brought back to the conversation when I saw Leon looking at me and I then began to panic that I should have answered a question which was asked ages ago.

"That's it I'm just about done, thanks for the cuppa"

I smiled, taking the mug from his hands.

"No worries, can I get you another?"

"No that's okay I better shoot as I've got another job I've got to get to"

He packed up his tools and was gone within the minute, my concentration was brought back to the mark on the floor.

The closer I got I could tell now that this mark was a footprint, the one thing that had me confused was the shape and the size. The tip was small and narrow , the heel wasn't too far away from the tip as though the size wasn't much bigger than a size 5. Was it a woman in here last night? I couldn't help but wonder what would a woman be after? I couldn't be sure whether it was a woman or not and the more I find, the less I feel I do know.

Friday 19th June 2018 18:28

I sat on the opposite side of the table to Emmett just waiting for the silence to be broken at the start of a conversation. I had no idea how long we'd sat in silence but we'd both nearly finished our dinner.

"How was your day today?"

"Yeah fine"

"That's good" I slowly placed my food in my mouth trying to start a conversation where he'd be interested.

"I.... I found a footprint by the door today did I tell you"

" Right? Now that's some exciting news"

"No, this footprint must have been from whoever was in here last night as I haven't had any shoes on all day"

"Well it must have been mine or the bloke who came to change the locks"

"Well you see that's the thing , this footprint was no man's footprint , this shoe was a small boot with a bit of a heel"

Emmett lifted his head up from the table looking at me intensely with curiosity.

"Isn't that strange , I mean what would a woman want with anything out of here , she certainly wouldn't find anything valuable of mine."

"Hmmmm , well the locks have been changed with just two keys , one for me and one for you so we have no worries of anyone getting in here now."

The conversation was rapidly changed as though the events were to be forgotten about. But I still felt as though there was more to this.

Saturday 20th June 2023 06:18

I managed to sleep right the way through the night, which was good considering my boss had sent me over some work to do from home so I can keep myself in the loop. I Felt as though things were gradually getting back to normal , whatever that was.

The day dawned bright and clear with a crisp wind yet the light of dawn seeped through the gap in the blinds giving me positive vibes for the day ahead. I got myself ready and bounded down the stairs to the table where Emmett had breakfast already made.

"What is all this?" I gasped with glee.

"Well I realise we haven't had much time together recently with me working such long hours plus you need a strong breakfast for all your work you've got to do today." He smiled with a childish grin.

"Awh, you're so sweet." I said whilst running over to kiss him.

"But can I just say this is definitely a woman's job."

"What makes you say that?" he looked despondent.

"Well you see the thing is, one of the vital parts of eating food is that you need plates , bowls and cutlery." I smiled with an arrogant look.

"Buggar , I knew I'd forgotten something."

"No, I'm only joking, don't worry , this is absolutely amazing, just what I need before a big day , thank you babe."

He just smiled back to feeling pleased.

"I'll get you a bowl."

"No, don't worry I'll get them, I'm making coffee anyway."

My smile turned to a confused frown from something that I was not expecting.

"Have you moved all the bowls and plates?"

"No why would I do that?" he laughed thinking I was joking.

"I spent all day yesterday arranging everything in the kitchen and the bowls and plates were in this cupboard here, so where have they been moved to?"

"I don't know babe , are you sure they're not in another one?"

I frantically started swinging the doors open until I found them on the opposite side to where I distinctly remember putting them yesterday.

"I don't understand why didn't you just tell me you'd moved them into this one?" I began to laugh.

"I haven't moved anything; I didn't even know where they were to get them out" he persisted to read from his newspaper.

The panic had set sail in my eyes , someone had been back in the house and now I realise this is becoming personal to me. Emmett wouldn't have noticed something like that, I believe that but someone knew I would , someone wants to scare me but what is it they

81

exactly want. Every time I feel the panic inside of me it turned to frustration, I began to feel so fed up of constantly fighting to stay in control of everything when really everything feels as though its falling apart.

Saturday 20th June 2018 17:38

I took a wonder to the shop to get some bits for tea after sitting at the dining room table all day but by the time I got back I noticed the door was unlocked and Emmett's car on the drive. I shouted up the stairs after looking all downstairs. I could see the shine of the light from upstairs, I wondered if Emmett had already gone to bed. I stepped lightly up the stairs intending to scare him awake, I got halfway upstairs before realising he wasn't asleep but was actually on the phone to someone who he seemed quite panicked about.

"That was far too close , you need to be careful next time."

I stood leant against the door just waiting for him to notice I was there. He eventually saw me when he frantically put the phone down and came over to me for a hug.

"What was all that about?"

"Oh…. Nothing, just someone at work forgot to write out paperwork which quite frankly we all could have got into shit for."

"Oh right, it sounded like you were worried I did wonder why."

"Anyway. How was your day of working from home?"

"Yeah, it was okay, very tired now though , any chance you'd like me to run me a bath?" I said, widening my eyes for a better chance.

"Of course I will" he walked off to run me a bath whilst I got caught up on folding the ironing.

I got in the bath while it was still running , I took comfort in the noises the tap made as the bath began to fill. I swirled the water around my fingers listening to the sound of the ripples overlapping towards the other side. The flicker of the candle crackled in the corner , as I just listened to all the noises my body began to unfold and relax. This was just what I needed.

Sunday 21st of June 2018 04:16

Scratch, scratch , scratch the relentless noise coming from outside. I tossed , turned and even put my pillow over my head but the noise wasn't going away. I was so sleep deprived as having no sleep was starting to catch up on me, I was becoming more and more paranoid.

I completely gave up on trying to sleep by this point and jumped abruptly to the window to get a clear view of the garden. I gently pushed the curtains to either side and glimpsed the outside view. I couldn't believe what I was seeing.

"Emmett get up, get up now"

There was no way he was missing this, as seen as though I've been the one to notice everything else.

"Why, what's up?" he sprung up from the bed.

"Just come quick" I shouted.

We bounded down the stairs and jumped to the floor, still quick on our feet we ran outside to the back hedges where I saw a person.

"There was someone stood the other side of the hedges I saw from the window" I shouted

Emmett opened the gate and ran down the alley to see if he could catch up.

"They've gone, they must have heard us shouting"

"We can't keep going on like this Emmett , I can't sleep I can't relax I'm so stressed all the time"

"Hey, hey it's okay I'll get someone to look at maybe getting a lock on the gate, would that be, okay?"

"We can't just keep putting locks on the problems Emmett I want something doing about this"

"Okay we'll speak about it tomorrow, let's go inside. It's cold out here."

He wrapped his arms around me tight which gave me a small amount of comfort, but I didn't know what the solution was at this point.

Monday 22nd June 2018 10:30

I sat quietly at the table , my eyes barely awake, just questioning what I needed to do next. Twice the door knocks, with a heavy and strong pound.

I was so tired that I tried to ignore the sound and wait for it to pass but I knew it wouldn't , I flicked my hair from within my eyes and slowly walked over to the door.

"Hello there"

A rush of anxiety flooded my body, I could feel the tension rising within me. After the pervious nights incident, why would this strange man be standing at me door? My instincts were to slam the door shut and lock it, but something about his demeanour made me realise there was nothing to fear. This was when I first met Dan the gardener that I'd already told you about.

I think something keeps going through my head about Emmett's attitude towards Dan. I don't know if its just my state of mind but I cant understand why Emmett was on the defensive about someone who was there to help.

Wednesday 24th June 2018 09:56

The last few days have been quiet ,and I'd never been so grateful for the sound of quiet. We'd spent the last few days putting up security and locks which gave me a feeling of safety. We also started to decorate the cottage which made me feel a bit for settled and at home, I put up photos and canvases, I even went out to get some gorgeous flowers and vases to colour theme each room . I was a bit on edge when I woke up this morning knowing that I was going to be on my own for the night as Emmett will be out for the night on a works course.

"Are you sure you'll be okay with this? , I'll cancel if you want me to"

"No I'll be fine honestly I've got the security and the locks, it's only one night at the end of the day." I tried to reassure him but also myself as I couldn't help but feel sick to my stomach.

I watched him haul his bags to the ford focus which was parked at the top of the lane.

"Now final check , are you sure you'll be okay?"

"Emmett I'll be fine ; I've got loads to be getting on with" the truth was , I didn't.

"Ring me if you need anything won't you?"

"Yeah of course I will , go on you'll be late if you don't get off soon."

"Okay love you"

"Love you too"

Wednesday 24th June 2018 20:24

After staring at the screen of the tv for hours on end I decided I was ready to take myself up to bed, for I was already falling asleep anyway.

I went around the house intensely checking the house , the windows , doors , locks and security.

I decided to put the radio on for the night for company. I hoped that the soothing noise would help me sleep as soon as I got into bed.

I was settled in for the night especially after doing all my checks, I think I'm going to sleep well tonight.

Thursday 25th June 2018 02:24

The noise downstairs can only be described as a whirlwind of explosive bangs , crashing at full blast against the wall. The relentless echoes of the crashes sent sirens through my ears. I knew I had to get up out of bed for I either go to them or they shall come to me. It had become routine for me to bound down the stairs and jump to the floor which this time I had come to terms with my worst nightmare.

There he stood in the doorway ,his hands clenched straining both his arms. He wore all black. His jacket is smooth textured , the kind of which you could hear each raindrop fall on. His darkly coloured jeans sat just on top of his boots. He slowly began to turn my way.

It was the same man I had seen earlier that week in the town, looking exactly the same.

I didn't give him a chance to look at my face, I ran out the backdoor into the alley towards the woods.

I still to this day don't know who found me but whoever it was must have seen what happened for I was laid in the darkness of the night in the middle of absolutely nowhere.

And this is where I began to run. Although I was running at speed it all felt like slow motion. My feet felt heavy as my quick paced run lead me turning and winding through the paths of the unknown. The tree branches felt like witches fingers grabbing out to catch me and entwine me into their clutches. I swear there was a ghostly howling sound coming from the distance, then I realised it was the heavy breathing of my pursuer. I could feel the energy lacking from my body the further I ran ; I was worried I was running out of time to keep myself going and to evade my tormentor. Eventually the running came to a stop and all I remember was the darkness.

I still to this day don't know who found me but whoever it was must have seen what happened for I was laid in the darkness of the night in the middle of absolutely nowhere.

Chapter 13

Freezing was the ground I was laid on, my dithering bones rattling to my core. The sound of leaves wisping through to my ears and the sound of the wind howling to the whales of despair I felt. I wasn't awake, nor was I asleep but neither did I know which I was closer to. My face stuck with cold blood to the floor picking up bits of mud which dusted my cheeks.

From the only corner of my eye, I could see out of, I could see a small coruscating light shine upon my skin. The light was so powerful that I couldn't see the person who appeared to notice me. He was friendly, I could tell by his gentle attempt to lift me into his arms. They were definitely a he, for his masculine distinctive smell was heavy in aroma but delicate to the skin.

I'd definitely come across this smell of combined stale cigarette smoke with the charms of his sweet aftershave. He walked with confidence by the slow pace he walked at and with every step came the squeak , the sound that wellies make when squeaking in the mud. This mystery man all of a sudden doesn't seem like a perfect stranger anymore....

"Daniel" my voice pleaded as though I was answering my own dream. I was still in the same hospital bed and by this point I had no idea how long I had been here for. I stripped myself from the multiple wires which were attached to all different parts of my body and stood upon my feet which is something I haven't done for a while.

I glanced over to where Melanie had been sitting but due to a high dose of medication I must have drifted off. I had no idea how long I'd been asleep but it didn't matter as suddenly everything was starting to make sense.

I swiftly packed up my things which seemed to be scattered across the whole room. I ran through to the bathroom, frantically putting everything in my bag. Just as I was about to step out of the room the mirror on the wall caught my eye, when was the last time I looked in the mirror?

I don't think anyone would be thinking I'm the fairest of them all. I had no time to patch myself up , there was somewhere important I knew I had to be.

Chapter 14

At the first glance, everything still looked the exact same from last time. The same cherry red door spaced in the middle of both flowered filled windows, a place so unfamiliar to everyone but me.

My head lay as far back on my seat as possible with no indication of me moving any time soon, yet my eyes ,still gazing out the windows of my car, were drawn towards the place I thought I'd never return to.

The wind pushed up against my car distracting my eyes from my intense stare, a dark shadowy figure was approaching me from behind , his silhouette shadowed the bright orange sunset which hooded the features of his face.

I waited for him to walk past to be sure.

"Daniel?"

"B, Beth is that you?" he said whilst frowning until he realised who was talking to him.

"Why did you lie?"

"Lie? What are you talking about?"

"I know it was you that night that found me and took me to wherever you did"

I began to walk away assuming that I'd never get an answer.

"No wait let me explain ,please?" he dragged my arm back to face him.

I reluctantly looked at him yet I knew curiosity would answer for me anyway.

"My house is just up the road. Please come in for a cuppa and I will explain everything"

He smiled promisingly.

How could I say no?

Chapter 15

Daniel filled our mugs with tea and finished them with just a splash of milk as I leaned against his kitchen side.

"Do you take sugar?" was the first thing he had said all the time I had been in his.

"Just one please" I replied.

"Shall we go through?" he wandered on through to his living room where I sat on the armchair opposite Daniel.

"I don't understand why didn't you tell me?"

"At first , I didn't think it was important considering I had no idea who you were. As far as I was concerned, I had just picked up a woman who was laid out in the cold and I had no idea why she was out there in the first place."

"so, you must have seen that man?"

"What man?"

"The man who chased me out of the cottage and all through the woods, he was the reason I was out there."

"I definitely didn't see anyone else out there"

"I'm a bit confused if I'm honest, how did you even find me out there at that time of night?"

"I'm going to start from the beginning, it may make a bit more sense.

"That night me and Melanie had got into a fight, if I'm honest it was one of many that week, I came home late therefore our argument was a late one. She left the house leaving the door wide open and drove off, which is when I saw you in the distance."

A long pause with a long breath was exchanged between the both of us.

"So, what about you? you didn't tell me you knew it was me" he sat up straight.

"I only remembered about an hour ago, I think talking to Melanie might have jogged my memory."

"When did you speak to Melanie?"

"When I was in hospital she came and spoke to me"

"You were in the hospital?"

"Oh yeah I had a bit of a funny turn the other night, I'm absolutely fine but I couldn't get in for my counselling session so I think Emmett arranged for her to come to me."

"Oh, I see"

"I'm sorry it must be a bit of a touchy subject"

"No, it's okay"

"It's just you seem to clam up whenever I mention her"

94

"There is probably something I should tell you"

I didn't respond only to look back up at him so he knew I was listening.

"Melanie's not who you think she is, I haven't actually got around to telling you why we split up"

"You don't need to tell me that if you don't want to Daniel"

He chose to ignore what I said and persisted to speak anyway.

"We'd been a bit off with each other for ages, I just assumed it was because we didn't see much of each other for a while because of work. But every night would become more strained and most nights she'd end up staying out late.

A few months later she'd told me that she wanted a divorce because she wasn't happy in our marriage anymore and that she'd found someone else. I knew it was coming because we barely saw each other anymore but I think it was definitely a shock when she said she'd met someone else.

It took a few days for it to sink in until I finally hit the roof about it, I found out who she'd been seeing and went round to his house. I have to say I was pretty angry and I'm ashamed to say how I behaved but, in that moment, it felt like I had no control over my emotions, I banged my fists against the door demanding for him to come out and meet me face to face. However, what I was next to see wasn't something I expected, a woman answered the door and told me about what Melanie had done.

She said Melanie had been harassing her trying to get her to leave her husband and how she had even broken into their house to try and scare her off. Her husband eventually found out what Melanie had been doing when he caught her in their house one night and confronted her, the couple eventually decided to move back into the city."

"When you say they moved back to the city...."

"They were the couple who lived in the cottage before you and Emmett moved in"

"So, you're telling me that she did this to the couple who lived in there before us?"

"Yes"

"Are you trying to tell me you think it was Melanie who kept coming into our cottage?"

"I'm not saying for definite but it is possible."

"No, no that can't be because I know I've been seeing a man"

"I don't know whether this is even connected but I just thought you should know"

"I'm going to go home and talk to Emmett I think that's the best thing to do"

"I don't want to scare you ; I'm just worried that's all"

"I know, and I'm glad you told me, I think I need to start getting some answers."

"I do too" he escorted me to the door and watched me leave and get into my car.

Chapter 16

I finally made it back to the flat but I wasn't sure if anyone was in. I then realised that I hadn't been here for a few days due to being in hospital which also made me realise I hadn't seen Emmett in days. I walked on through to the bedroom where Emmett was in fact in.

"Why are you here?"

"Oh, nice to see you too "I slightly laughed with a shocked face.

"No, I just meant I thought you were in hospital; they didn't tell me that you could leave?"

"What do you mean?"

"Well I asked them to ring me when they said you could leave"

"Well, I felt much better so I decided to leave, which I'm glad I did because I've just been to see someone"

"Okay, and who was that?"

"I went to see Daniel who has just told me something which is really important I tell you."

"Okay?"

I sat on the bed next to Emmett and looked deeply into his eyes and told him word for word what Daniel told me.

"So, what do you think, do you think this could be connected?"

"I think maybe you should change councillors so then we cut ties everywhere"

"Yeah, I agree , in a way it makes me feel a bit better knowing that I can do something about this"

I felt the most relaxed then I had in ages. I actually just laid back on the bed and just started to laugh.

"What are you laughing at? "Emmett laid next to me and joined in with me laughing.

"I just can't believe how stupid I've been"

"Well, I have to say it's nice to see a smile on your face" he said, smiling at me for the first time in ages.

"But I wouldn't let it go to your head. For all we know it could be a perfect stranger" he quickly contradicted himself.

"I know but if it is that means we can do something about it."

"Okay, whatever makes you feel better"

"Since I'm home, do you fancy doing us some dinner?"

"I think I can stretch to that; I'll sort something out whilst you unpack your bags"

He walked down into the kitchen still talking to me about all the things I've missed in 2 days and I found myself replying to things I couldn't even hear what he was saying.

I started by unpacking my clothes and folding them at the bottom of our wardrobe which is when I realised, we still need to properly unpack after getting back from the cottage. I found a blue sturdy carrier bag which I was certain wasn't in there a few days ago. Mind you I probably wouldn't be able to tell the fact that it was tucked right in the corner. I reached over and brought the bag closer to me.

I peered my head inside the bag, which is something I'd regret for the rest of my life. Inside was a pair of black workers boot, a dark reflective raincoat and a pair of dark-coloured jeans.

I heard the heavy footsteps piling up the stairs and yet I still wasn't making any effort to put everything back and pretend I never saw anything, as though my body froze still.

"you know I was thinking…" Emmett was cut off by himself noticing my still gaze at this blue bag.

There was many moments of silence as though an excuse was in the process of being made.

"Beth" he finally said.

"No, no you do not get to justify whatever your about to say", I ran into the ensuite starting to pack my bits up together , not really thinking of the next steps or where I'm really going to go.

"Just let me explain" he said whilst following me frantically through the house.

I paused to look at him straight in the eyes and in that moment I realised , I don't think I know him at all.

"It was just so easy Beth , your so easily lead and so easy to manipulate, at first I thought this was a bad idea and I actually felt quite bad for putting you through everything I did but then Melanie decided we should persist with the plan, and once I saw how easily you believed that you were just going mad I never thought you'd expect any different.

"Melanie , I should have known , I knew there was something going on there but I never expected anything on this level and for my own husband to put me through all of this.

I looked into his eyes from mine which where water logged with the heart heavy tears, I've never looked into his eyes and felt betrayal before and yet right here in this moment all I could see was this monster who used me to get exactly what he wanted.

"So that's it? you did all this because you want to be with Melanie."

"Well it's not just about that"

"How long?" I responded with the quickest thing I could think of.

"It's not important"

"How long Emmett? How long have you and Melanie been a thing? I bellowed from the other side of the room demanding an answer.

"Since we moved into the cottage." he sheepishly replied.

"She told me about her divorce and from then we just hit it off as I think we both got each other."

"Well, that makes so much more sense as to why you never really liked Daniel."

"I could see him for who he was, he was trying to get into your pants Beth and Melanie said he'd probably come after you."

"I loved you Emmett , I would never have looked at someone that way , so it shouldn't have mattered what others thought of me.

"And I did love you too"

"Just not enough" he never replied after that , and that's when I realised this really was it for us.

He never said a word just looked at me with such a vindictive smug smile , I never realised how manipulative he was and how he was so controlled with such a clever or-castrated plan, he lead me to believe that I was going insane and I fully felt as though I had lost all control. I stood on the spot completely terrified from the person I thought was protecting me the most and id never felt that way before. All the months of frustration, fear and upset all boiled down to what I'd do next.

"I'll be honest this was never my plan, I was happy to just tell you what I wanted, you have to believe that." He said with no remorse just to probably make himself feel better.

"Do you know what that makes you?" I slowly walked up to him still with streaks of tears perched on my cheeks but now I could feel the tears falling quicker as the anger ran through my whole body.

"What?" he said with looking down at my face which was a few centimetres from his.

" A fucking coward. You didn't pick the hard way out, you chose to make me feel so worthless and try and destroy my life ,well let me tell you something, you didn't destroy my life , for anything you saved me from someone I clearly never truly knew so maybe I should be thanking you before I carried on committing my life to you."

As much as that satisfied me to say that to him , inside I was hurting so much and I still couldn't really believe what had just happened in the last half an hour. I picked up the rest of my things which didn't take long considering I hadn't started unpacking from being in hospital.

Before I walked out the door for the last time I turned around to take one last look at the flat and also one last look at Emmett who was standing in the doorway of the room by the door, I couldn't stand here any longer as I might convince myself I was dreaming and that this was another nightmare when really I knew that this was as real as it was going to get.

I ran as fast as I did that night as though I were re-living everything all over again , but this time I was running from someone I never thought I'd be running from.

I drove around for what felt like hours screaming all the frustration out from inside of me. I drove around in circles until I found myself leaving town and driving on the twisty roads of the countryside. I knew exactly where I was going to end up.

I walked out into the downpour of rain which poured onto my face like the streaks of cold tears dripping off my nose. My eyes stung with every deep tear that coursed down my face as though they were running like the flow of the sea. The anger boiled inside of me and yet I felt nothing, I wasn't even sure how to react to such a cold betrayal.

I walk over to the bench that looks out onto the beautiful midnight blue sea which was lit up in spirals and circles from the moon and stars. The rain drizzled and dripped onto the water in an enticing serenade which fascinated me to sit and watch. My whole body was filled with goosebumps making my body shiver from my shoulders down to my toes. The more I sat and gazed into the wonders of the water the more I realised I had no plan , no place to stay and nothing but a bag of clothes which were closest to me.

I decided to get back up and walk eventually reaching a destination but still not sure where that would be. My clothes were so waterlogged they began to feel so heavy and my shoes squelched with every step. I finally reached another cottage ; I'd forgotten how far apart and spread out they are. I was reluctant to knock as most people are in bed at early hours of the morning.

I tried quietly to open the gate which squeaked to the sound of the wind, despite everything I couldn't help but notice how pretty this garden is and how the beautiful sites of reds, pinks and purples of flowers gave me a hint of a smile. I reached the door which I shyly knocked on hoping an angry person wasn't going to appear on the other side. The door slowly opened to a very familiar face.

"Bethany?"

"Daniel... I'm so sorry did I wake you?"

"No of course not I'm more bothered as to why you're out at this hour on your own"

"I can't go home"

"Well you better come in and get warm, I'll make you a cuppa"

I stepped in already feeling the warmth of Daniels glowing kindness, up until this point I never realised how much he's been there for me. And in such a small space of time I had almost forgot what even happened tonight.

Chapter 17

4 **years later**

Before I walked my way down the aisle, I took one last look around. I was holding the most beautiful bouquet of flowers full of pink and lavender. My dress to match the flowers was beautiful in a lilac and crystal white pearls twisted into my brunette curls. I matched the other six bridesmaids who followed in a clique of pastel purple , all apart from the bride in gorgeous white with a veil cascading down to her beautiful satin white pumps.

"Are you ready for this?"

"I really am Beth"

"I'm so happy for you Pops"

"This will be you in the next year, how do you feel about that?"

I'm still getting over the fact I have a toddler and a newborn ; I never saw that coming"

We both instantly looked down to my daughter Tiara who was clutching onto my hand not having a clue what was going on.

"I wonder if Timothy's settled in there , you might have to walk down the aisle to a screaming baby"

"Of course he'll be okay he's with your lovely fiancé and his perfect daddy"

Just as we were staring to get into conversation the doors swung open to all the eyes of the standing people in the benches waiting for the bridesmaids to walk down the aisle to see the blushing bride. Me and Tiara were right at the back of the congregate right in front of poppy, as I am the maid of honour she wanted me right next to her however I don't think either of us would have planned that I would have had a daughter who is also a bridesmaid.

We slowly walked down the aisle in our pairs , walking to the rhythm of the piano. I reached about half way and that's where I saw him as best man right at the front, holding on to our newborn son Timothy . I knew today wasn't about me but I couldn't help imagining when I walk own that isle I'll be there next to him forever and always. I smiled over to him where he rebounded his smile that shone like all the stars in the sky.

After the groom and bride sealed their vows with their kiss the whole room got up to cheer and applauded and even throw confetti if there was any left from the kids eating their way through them. Poppy and Henry walked out hand in hand happily married.

"Hey"

"Hey , I can't believe how handsome both my boys are"

"And I can't believe how absolutely gorgeous both my girls are"

I smiled with complete content and glee.

"I can't believe this will be us next year , and I truly can't wait to call you my wife"

"I can't wait either"

"I love you Beth"

"I love you Daniel"

About the author

Annie is seventeen years old and first found a passion for writing after going along to a local writing group in Cleethorpes with her mum, this gave her confidence to branch out and start writing her own things. Annie wrote this novel whilst taking her GCSES.

Annie likes to read a variety of different genres from supernatural to thrillers.

She currently at college studying criminology and Double uniformed protective services.

Her other interests are Irish dancing , sport and fitness, walking and listening to music and crafts.

Annies two best friends are her sausage dogs Danny and Tommy.

Acknowledgements

First of all, I'd like to thank my wonderful best friend , my mum. Not only are you my biggest supporter in everything I do, but you give me the courage to take on things I would of never of thought to be possible. You truly are my inspiration. Thanks mum.

I'd also like to thank the globe coffee shop for hosting such amazing writing nights and making me feel really welcome into the group.

And finally thank you to all the globe members I have made some awesome friends.

Printed in Great Britain
by Amazon

38145048R00066